Go, Bots! Go!

Just Right Reader Inc.

The bots have a match.
The task is to win.

Buzz - Saw - Bot can cut.
Fin - Bot can chomp.

Who will win?

1

"Go, bots. Go!" yells the ref.

Buzz - Saw - Bot is fast. Zip! It wants to bump Fin - Bot, but that bot chomps.

Crunch!

Fin - Bot wants to stump Buzz - Saw - Bot.

3

Buzz - Saw - Bot wants to flip Fin - Bot over.

Buzz - Saw - Bot thumps away, but it can't flip it!

Fin - Bot is going in for a chomp. It is quick!

This match is a thrill!

Will Fin - Bot crush Buzz - Saw - Bot?

Buzz - Saw - Bot has one trick left.

Buzz - Saw - Bot dashes and cuts. It is a risk, but Buzz - Saw - Bot wants to win. Buzz - Saw - Bot is going for it!

9

They crash in a big romp!

Buzz - Saw - Bot cuts. It is strong and lifts Fin - Bot up.

Fin - Bot crashes down!

Will Fin - Bot get back up?

No, it will not!

The ref yells, "Buzz - Saw - Bot wins the match!"

Buzz - Saw - Bot is the champ!

Ending Blends -sk, -mp

Blending Fun

- These words have ending blends! Some of them have beginning blends or digraphs. Try sounding them out.

- Say each word three times to blend the sounds smoothly!

brisk	grump
champ	stamp
desk	whisk

Decodable Words

bump	romp
champ	stump
chomp	task
risk	thump

High-Frequency Words

give	saw
now	some
one	they

Decodable Words can be sounded out based on the letter-sound relationships.

High-Frequency Words are the most commonly used words. Note: For Sets 21 - 40, the words listed above do not all appear in every book.

Blends are two adjoining consonants that each make their own sounds, like /m/ /p/ in lamp.